Tigers & Tea with Toppy

A TRUE ADVENTURE IN
NEW YORK CITY
WITH WILDLIFE ARTIST
CHARLES R. KNIGHT,
WHO LOVED SABER-TOOTHED CATS,
PARTIES AT THE PLAZA,
AND PEOPLE AND ANIMALS
OF ALL STRIPES

BY **Barbara Kerley**
AUTHOR OF *THE DINOSAURS OF WATERHOUSE HAWKINS*

WITH **Rhoda Knight Kalt**
GRANDDAUGHTER OF CHARLES R. KNIGHT

ILLUSTRATIONS BY **Matte Stephens**
WITH ORIGINAL ARTWORK BY CHARLES R. KNIGHT

SCHOLASTIC PRESS  NEW YORK

Fridays are the best days of the week.
That's when Rhoda begins her weekends with
Grandpa Toppy!

As soon as school lets out, she meets him
at one of their favorite places: the
American Museum of Natural History.

Hand in hand, they roam
vast halls filled with Toppy's paintings.
Toppy is the famous wildlife artist Charles R. Knight.

His paintings were some of the first to show people what
prehistoric animals looked like. As Toppy tells Rhoda
stories about each creature, they seem to come
alive! And she feels the magic of traveling
to an ancient world.

Rhoda and Toppy walk by dinosaur
and woolly mammoth fossils to his favorite:
the saber-toothed cat.

"Those fangs are scary!" says Rhoda.
"You couldn't have him as a pet!" Toppy says.

Toppy has been coming
to the museum
since he was
five years old.

"It was heaven
for a boy who loved
all kinds of wildlife,"
he tells Rhoda.

"When I first decided to be an animal painter, I spent most of my time here," he tells Rhoda as they explore the museum's taxidermy workshop. "It's one of the best places in the world to really learn something about animal anatomy."

To be a really good artist, Toppy had to study how each animal is "put together" — how its bones, joints, and muscles work in harmony.

He discovered all kinds of things: A chimp's shoulder blades lie across its back, while an elephant's jut straight up.

A tiger flattens its ears and bares its teeth
when alarmed.

A gorilla walks on
the edges of its feet

and a dog walks on
its toes.

Toppy noted everything.

Tiger flattens ears.

The more Toppy looked and learned, the better his art became, until one special day in 1894. When he was only twenty years old, the museum asked him to create a painting of a prehistoric animal. For the first time, Toppy didn't have a complete animal to study, only fossil remains. The *Elotherium* bones, he noticed, resembled a modern-day pig. He examined the skeleton carefully. Then he carried all that he'd learned about animals . . .

. . . and stepped into the past.

After saying goodbye to the *Elotherium* and
lots of other creatures, Rhoda and Toppy head home
for a nice dinner with Grandma Nonnie.
Then Nonnie turns on the radio, and Toppy works
on his book about how to draw animals.

He holds the paper close. Even though
his eyes are very weak now, he still sees things
that other artists miss. He erases a line and
tries again. He wants to teach
young artists all that he has learned.

In the morning, while Nonnie gets ready to go to the market, Rhoda and Toppy set out for the Central Park Zoo. Rhoda takes Toppy's hand and guides him as they stroll down West 59th Street. They always stop to feed the horses on their way.

At the zoo, Rhoda and Toppy like to make sure
the animals are happy and well.

Rhoda sings to the sea lions.
She blows kisses to the monkeys.
She even helps the zookeeper
feed the polar bears.

Of course,
they visit the big cats — and
Toppy's favorite, the tiger.

Toppy can't see him very well anymore,
but Toppy knows a tiger by heart.
"Look at the intensity of his eyes," he tells Rhoda.
"Look at that beautiful stripe."

People often gather to listen to Toppy.
Toppy loves company, so he invites them home for tea.

Nonnie never knows how many people
Toppy will bring home, so she always has plenty of everything.
Rhoda feels very grown-up serving the sandwiches
and chatting with everyone, just like Nonnie.

But her favorite part of the tea party is when Toppy puts on his smock, heads to his easel, and picks up his palette and brush.

He daubs a touch of white, a little more brown,
carefully mixing until the color is perfect.
Rhoda knows how hard he works
to get each painting just right.

In the evening, as Toppy settles in to work on his book,
Rhoda snuggles into her sofa bed in Toppy's studio.
She hopes that one day she will find something she loves
as much as he loves drawing and painting animals.

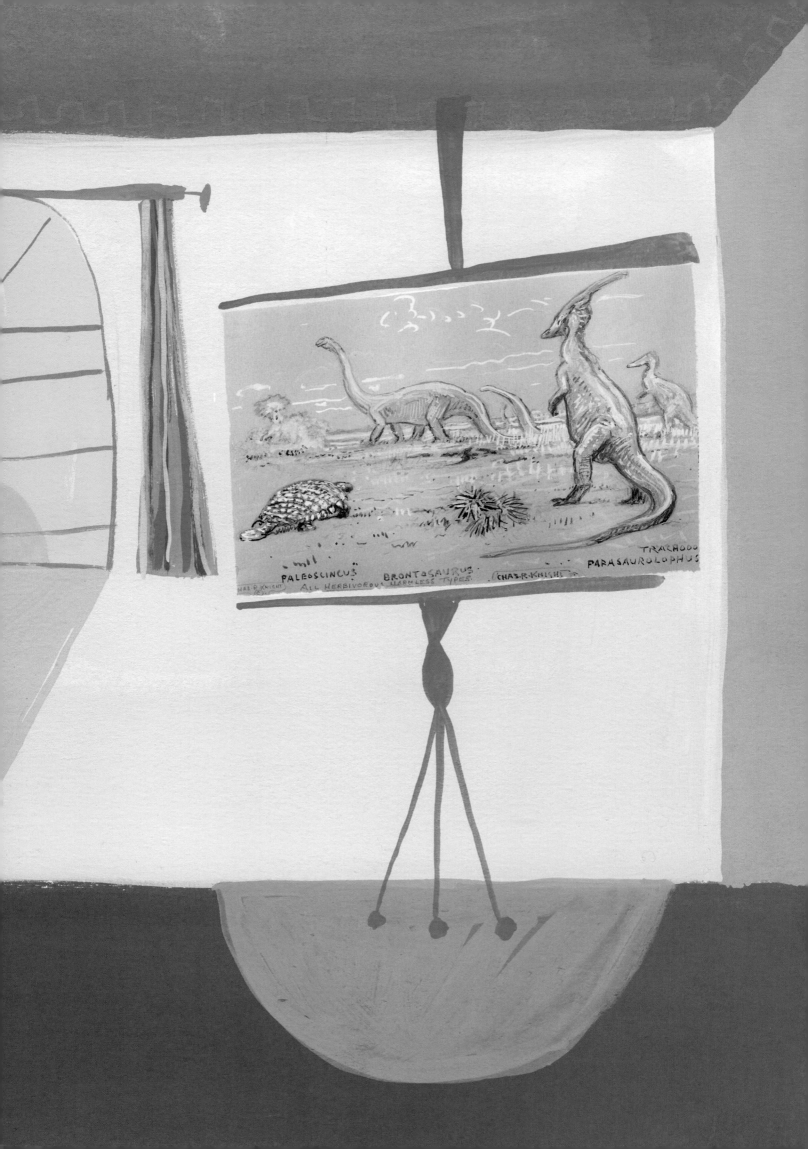

**So on Sunday morning, over big bowls of oatmeal,
Rhoda asks Toppy *how* she will find what she loves best.**

It's simple, Toppy tells her:

"Always follow your heart."

And right now, Toppy knows what his heart wants.
The drawings he's been working on all weekend are almost done,
and that calls for a celebration. He invites Rhoda and Nonnie
out for tea at The Palm Court of The Plaza Hotel!
Rhoda and Nonnie hurry to get ready.

Then Rhoda races down the hall to get her purse.
"Ready!" says Rhoda.
"We're off!" Toppy says.

Rhoda doesn't know yet what
she loves best. She doesn't know
where her heart will lead her.
But she carries Toppy's stories
and all that he has taught her . . .

. . . and Rhoda skips ahead.

AUTHOR & ARTIST NOTES

In the late 1880s, when Charles R. Knight was about fourteen, he left general studies to go to art school, delighted to put homework — and geometry — behind him.

Over the next few years, he learned about light, contours, and shadow with "tremendous zest and enthusiasm."

By the time he was sixteen, he was helping design stained glass windows for churches. Soon he was illustrating books and magazine articles.

But he never stopped drawing animals, especially the big cats at the Central Park Zoo. "Lions and tigers were always my favorites," he recalled in his autobiography. "I learned to be careful when I was working as the claws of a tiger can do terrific damage unless one is very watchful."

He returned again and again to the American Museum of Natural History. Even though he was still a teenager, Knight soon became friends with the men working in the taxidermy department, who loved — as he did — uncovering "the secrets of animal anatomy."

Knight "drew close-ups of noses, eyes, paws, and ears." He studied the muscles and bones.

And when he went to the Central Park Zoo, and later, the Bronx Zoo, he found that these studies gave him "a far deeper insight" into the animals he drew as they "moved about in their cages."

It was this early and concentrated study that allowed him in 1894 to look at the fossilized skeleton of the prehistoric *Elotherium* (now more commonly known as *Entelodon*) and visualize the once-living animal — opening up "a whole new field of research and study" into which he "could delve," he discovered, to his "heart's content."

Knight did just that, creating amazing paintings and murals for the next forty years. His vivid and lifelike depictions — displayed next to the American Museum of Natural History's extensive collection of fossils — seemed to bring these long-extinct creatures to life. He began his career at the Museum, mentored by two legendary paleontologists: Edward Drinker Cope and Henry Fairfield Osborn. Knight continued his pioneering work for the Field Museum in Chicago and other esteemed institutions, inspiring generations of scientists and artists and helping to shape our understanding of and appreciation for prehistoric animals. His accomplishments are all the more remarkable when you consider that for much of his life, he was legally blind. Even though he was visually impaired, his talent and vision have shown us a world we might never have otherwise been able to see or imagine.

In addition to his profound contributions to the fields of art and animal science, Charles R. Knight's life and work remind us of the importance of dedication, determination, and always following your heart.

As a young girl, Rhoda was lucky to have received such wisdom and love from Toppy. And I was lucky to experience those gifts firsthand through my countless email exchanges and hours of conversation with Rhoda, whose memories and stories keep Toppy's spirit very much alive.

—BARBARA KERLEY

⠀⠀⠀‖‖ ‖‖ ‖‖

I have a very particular approach to creating my artwork. My poor eyesight prevents me from simply taking a paintbrush and putting it to canvas. I have to use special lights so I can see everything properly, and a magnifying glass to get all the details just right, even with my very thick eyeglasses. Sound familiar? Charles R. Knight did almost the same thing his entire career. In order to draw or paint, he had to put his face so close to the paper or canvas that he was practically touching it. My editor wasn't aware of our shared impairments when she hired me for this project; it just turned out to be one of those "art imitates life" moments.

In creating the illustrations for the book, I relished the opportunity to study the work of a true virtuoso. But what has struck me the most over these past several months are Knight's spectacular paintings of dinosaurs. They are as lifelike as any skeleton or replica I've seen in person, and have the effect of transporting me across millions of years. I hope my work has brought to life the talent, passion, and charisma of this important artist and inspires you to seek out more of his work, and to respect the natural world and all its creatures as he did.

—MATTE STEPHENS

Some of my finest childhood memories are of visiting my beloved grandfather Toppy and my grandmother Annie Hardcastle Knight, or Nonnie, as I called her, in their cozy apartment in the middle of Manhattan.

Toppy and I had so many great adventures! At the American Museum of Natural History, we'd roam the halls together, and I'd marvel as he pointed out the fossils and all the different kinds of skeletons. Sometimes, when Toppy worked with the Museum staff, I even got to help clean the fossils, which was very exciting. Toppy discussed art with everyone we encountered — from Museum staff to art students and perfect strangers who had no idea they were chatting with the Museum's most distinguished artist. I remember how amazed they were when he would gently guide their pencils to capture an animal's posture or facial expression.

On Saturdays, we visited the animals at the Central Park Zoo, with particular attention paid to the sick animals. Toppy wanted to ensure they were getting the proper care. He regarded all the animals as his friends, and I can recall a time when a yak fell sick — my grandfather was so distraught I thought he needed a sick day himself.

Then there were our visits to The Plaza Hotel!

Nonnie and I would dress up, and I would sing and dance up the steps of the hotel. I remember feeling so grown-up as I sipped tea with Toppy and Nonnie at the famous Palm Court.

But perhaps best of all was when Toppy would tell me a story. Wherever we happened to be, he would invariably turn to me and spin a wonderful tale of animals, and traveling, and family. I remember being so mesmerized that it would take me a while to notice a crowd gathering around us, each person hanging on Toppy's every word. When he told these stories or talked to me about animal behavior at the zoo, people always drew closer to listen. In these interactions, Toppy would really get to know those around him, and afterward would even invite a few people home for tea. Often, they became his lifelong friends.

The stories I could tell you about my grandfather are endless. In these pages, I hope I have given you a taste of those enchanted years and the magical weekends Toppy, Nonnie, and I spent together, and that you have enjoyed the book. If you are able to share it with a grandparent of your own, that would be most special of all. And I hope you always follow your heart, as Toppy did and as I have in dedicating my life to preserving his legacy.

—RHODA KNIGHT KALT

SOURCES & ACKNOWLEDGMENTS

All quotes in the book are drawn from interviews with Rhoda Knight Kalt, with the exception of the following:

Page 10: "It was heaven . . .": Rhoda Knight Kalt, "Nonnie and Toppy: An Affectionate Memoir," *Prehistoric Times*, Summer 2013, 11.

Page 11: "shapes and figures": Charles R. Knight, *Animal Drawing: Anatomy and Action for Artists* (New York: Dover Publications, Inc. 1947), 90.

Page 12: "character": (Knight, *Animal Drawing*, 70).

Page 12: "weight, grace, and power": (Knight, *Animal Drawing*, 92).

Page 13: "When I first . . .": Kalt, *Prehistoric Times*, 19.

Page 14: "put together": (Knight, *Animal Drawing*, 90).

Page 42: "tremendous zest . . .": Charles R. Knight, *Autobiography of an Artist* (Ann Arbor: G. T. Labs, 2005), 18.

Page 42: "Lions and . . ." and "I learned . . .": (Knight, *Autobiography*, 34).

Page 42: "the secrets . . .": (Knight, *Autobiography*, 37).

Page 42: "drew close-ups . . .": (Knight, *Autobiography*, 39).

Page 42: "a far . . ." and "moved about . . .": (Knight, *Autobiography*, 39).

Page 42: "a whole new . . ." and "could delve . . .": (Knight, *Autobiography*, 40).

Page 44: Adapted from "How One Paints and Models an Animal" from *Animal Drawing: Anatomy and Action for Artists* by Charles R. Knight.
    Copyright © 1947 by Charles R. Knight. Published by Dover Publications, Inc. New York.

All of Charles R. Knight's original drawings, paintings, and photos — on pages 6–7, 20, 31, 33, 45, 46–47 — courtesy of Rhoda Knight Kalt.

Skeleton on page 17 and *Entelodon* (*Elotherium*) on pages 18–19 reprinted courtesy of the American Museum of Natural History.

ADAPTED FROM
"HOW ONE PAINTS AND MODELS AN ANIMAL"
BY CHARLES R. KNIGHT

There are many things to think about before one ever sets pencil to paper.

To begin with I should suggest a trip to a museum, where a close scrutiny of a mounted skeleton and a good anatomy book will acquaint you with the special characters of the creature you wish to represent.

Try something comparatively simple, a quietly resting creature of some sort, not a fast-moving, brightly colored and patterned tiger or leopard.

Observe at once and very carefully the silhouette. This exact shape is tremendously important; without it all your later work will be practically wasted.

The feet or head of your model must not be too large or too small. Also, be searching in your scrutiny of the shape of the feet and legs.

The joints and their proportionate size and position will next occupy your attention. All mammals have approximately the same number of joints. They may, however, vary in distance from one another and in the particular way in which they function.

Each group of animals has its special series of actions in running, walking, reclining, drinking, fighting, eating, etc. We may be sure, for example, that all the cats will do things in the same way. Horses, asses, and zebras have their own special action; cattle, sheep, goats, deer, and antelopes seem governed by a closely related series of movements; elephants stand widely apart from all the rest; camels and llamas follow along parallel lines in any movement they attempt.

In some creatures the effect of unusual hair disposal [placement] and very complicated color patterns make correct observation of the true shape almost impossible. Leopards and tigers are so covered by a maze of spots and stripes that a beginner in the art is left completely at sea. Study the plan of these patterns before putting it down.

You should acquaint yourself at least superficially with the psychological traits of the particular type of creature on which you are working.

Read books on the subject of animals in a wild state, their habits and environment and all other data concerning them. Such reading will stimulate and interest you and give you much insight into animals' special modes of existence, all of which will be a help when you come to draw them.

For Rhoda —BK

To all the young readers out there — always follow your heart —RKK

To my wife and our pets, for their endless inspiration —MS

Special thanks to Richard Milner, whose book for adults, *Charles R. Knight: The Artist Who Saw Through Time* (New York: Abrams, 2012), was enormously helpful in the writing of this book; to Tom Baione at the American Museum of Natural History Library for his invaluable assistance and fact-checking; to Melissa Knight Kalt, and most of all to Nonnie and to Toppy, who need no further introduction.

llll llll llll

llll llll llll

1–3. Pencil drawings of lions by Charles R. Knight, including "Toby," made at Antwerp Zoo in Belgium in 1896. • 4. Knight paints a portrait of "Sultan" at the Bronx Zoo in 1906. • 5. Knight creates a clay model of *Stegosaurus* in 1899. • 6. Knight's drawing of *Dimetrodon*. • 7. Knight's self-portrait in pencil circa 1892. • 8. Rhoda Knight Kalt about eight years old in New York City. • 9. Knight works on a painting of the Ice Age for AMNH. • All these photographs and drawings are from the collection of Rhoda Knight Kalt.

CHAS. R. KNIGHT

1

TOBY
ANTWERP ZOO.
1896.
C. R. KNIGHT

2

CHAS. R. KNIGHT

3

4

5

6

7

8

9

CHAS·R·KNIGHT
©·45